Lost in the DARKNESS OF THOUGHT

A Poetic Journey into the Depths of the Unknown

The forthcoming of morning is but the light of day,
The forthcoming of evening is but only the light taken away!

ROBERT R. BLONDIN

ARPress
ILLUMINATING IDEAS.
EMPOWERING VOICES

ARPress
45 Dan Road Suite 5
Canton MA 02021

Hotline: 1(888) 821-0229
Fax: 1(508) 545-7580

Ordering Information:
Quantity sales. Special discounts are available on quantity purchases by corporations, associations, and others. For details, contact the publisher at the address above.

Printed in the United States of America.

ISBN-13:   Softcover   979-8-89356-074-9
            Hardcover   979-8-89356-071-8
            eBook   979-8-89356-072-5

Library of Congress Control Number: 2024904002

Rev. date: 5/4/2019

Contents

Dedication

Dedicated to my family: my son Kyle (+Jessica, Austin, Sydney Marie & Jake) and my daughter Melinda (+Bruzlin & Nathaniel), *and to any other grandchildren that may come to be*, and to my Mom & Dad, Brothers & Sisters (see photo below).

The Blondin Family

Front: Leona (Daniher)
2nd Row: Louis, William (Dad), Evelyn (Mom), Reta (Oglestone), Joan (Windsor)
Back: Rolland, Leonard, Lloyd, Jack, Billy, Isabel (Whittaker), Robert, Edward

~ God Bless All ~

Preface

This book was written as a spinoff of my first book - this time as a short story with a poetic dark twist! All purely fun and fiction!

The book was concocted solely using some of my poetry and enhanced into a story telling venture, wherein I am lost in the darkness of thought.

There are characters suggested in this book, however they are indirect or unknown and reference may only be by name or by nickname or just simply to remain unknown.

Throughout the book there may be a few motivational type messages, take them for what they are worth.

Permit yourself to wander and to wonder as you enter a poetic journey into the depths of the unknown.

Intro

- storytelling with a poetic twist
- a short nap
- can't wake up
- hard to breathe
- can't think, can't remember
- almost complete darkness
- must find a way to escape
- need to get back to reality
- is this an out of body experience
- am I dead or am I still alive

Spent a long hard day trying to fix the outdated electrical system at an old dingy rundown hotel and now it is time to relax, maybe take a nap.

Just A Nap

I fixed a few loose electrical wires at the job I was on today, got myself zapped a few times too, but that was mainly because the hotel had a really ancient system which kept flickering and shorting out; just the normal everyday hazards of an electrician's job.

Otherwise, it was a pretty normal day; nothing seemed all that strange. Everything seemed to be restored, so I left for home.

No one was here, no one in sight; oh so quiet it be; I decided to rest my eyes, just for a second or two, just a short snooze.

Activities of the day kept running over and over in my head, repeating every now and then, even things I didn't remember doing, surfaced to and fro, all of it quickly spiraling and spinning out of control, some of it so new, some of it so old.

Then suddenly everything went dark, I mean really dark, pitch black.

I tried to wake up but I couldn't move, couldn't open my eyes, blackness ensued; seems like I'm in another body, floating askew, maybe I'm in another world I never knew.

Am I having a bad dream, with some nightmarish scheme?

Am I dead? Or am I still alive? Or is this just all in my head.

Darkness prevails; there is nothing I can do, nothing at all could stop the dread.

I can't move, can't lift my head, seems like I'm unconscious, in some kind of dark coma, in a dreamland of existence I never knew.

Realm Of Darkness

How did I get here? If only I knew what here was!

I can barely see, darkness fills the air, seems like a dark purplish mist permeates the surroundings, so hard to breathe, the mist saturates my being.

Hey, come on, what is this? What the hell is this?

Damn, maybe that's exactly where I am!

How can this be? Am I in a dream or is this real?

I remember closing my eyes, I remem.... ?

What the ? I can't remember anything, nothing, zilch, it's like I'm in a trance.

How? What? It doesn't make sense.

This is not just a dream, it's a bloody nightmare!

Who am I? Can't remember, can't remember.

I'm drawing a total blank, amnesia maybe, did I hit my head or something.

I have to wake up; I have to find a way out, help me, someone, anyone?

What do I do? I need to find a clue.

It seems like I'm in a world without light, a realm of darkness it be.

I can't see enough to even budge; should I try to move, should I even dare?

Through faded vision I can see a few tunnels of some kind directly ahead, like passageways; barely enough light to see.

It's a massive wall with six openings; I manage to move and take the first one to proceed.

I wonder what I'll find.

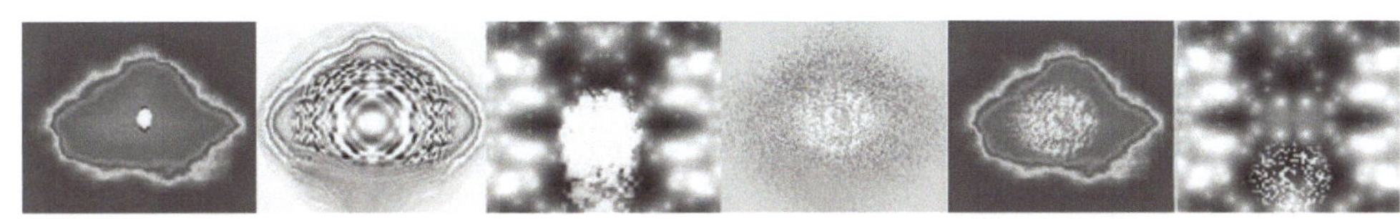

Cylinders Of Darkness

Where am I now? Feels like I'm in a vacuum, all kinds of things circling over my head, all quickly changing and rearranging, all in a flash of despair.

I attempt to go back but a barrier prevents this. Looks like I can only go one way, something's amiss.

My thoughts become muffled and distorted to a degree. Are they even my thoughts I'm thinking, is it even me?

Awaiting destiny, caressing each breath I have left; I know I'm hoping for more, much more, but nothing is emerging, nothing coming forth.

Why can't I wake up?

Nothing but time; am I just awaiting an end, the decisive end, a finality of sorts.

I see cylinders of darkness, tunnels of flickering light, peaking to the inevitable, as I go through a circular motion of life, then absolutely nothing, nothing but time, only time.

As seconds pass, there is the sound of broken glass; feels like the shattering of time, inflicting a sharp jagged pain, leaving an aching in my heart, that just won't seem to pass.

I'm lost in the darkness of thought? Is this just a dream or the ultimate nightmare, I am so caught?

How do I escape this non-reality? Is it just going to get worse? Or, is this maybe a dark embedded curse.

More dark tunnels ahead, only five openings this time. Strange!

For some reason I can only enter the first one, the others have an invisible barrier of sorts, preventing my run.

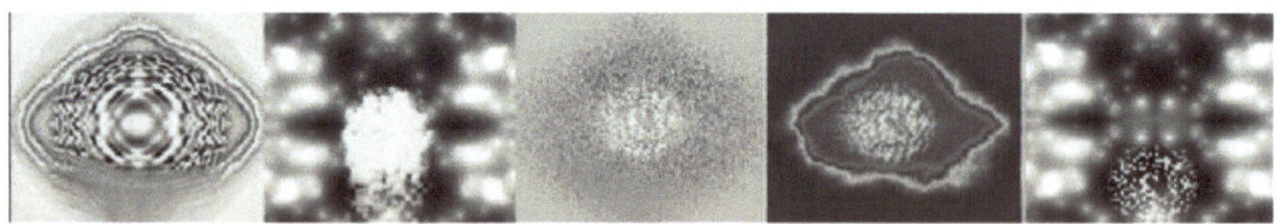

Only Time

I seem to be my own fugitive, waiting to recapture reality. Seems that my memory has escaped, but I haven't.

Some thoughts of my past slowly emerge but disappear so fast; just faded memories too.

And are they even my memories?

Why can't I just wake up?

The utter truth is I'm just sitting here in darkness, not knowing who I am, not knowing where I am or why I am even here.

Wish I knew what was happening, why me, why me?

Now falling into slow motion, with a sudden thud, I'm caught in the hands of time, unable to converse.

Now charred with fear, I hear the sounds of footsteps near.

But, nothing, nobody… not a soul!

All I see is cylinders of darkness, tunnels of dimmed light, with spiraling shadows, in and out of sight.

I seem to be surrounded by an aura, a mysterious aura, with a strange smell, maybe the scent of fresh cut flowers, yet, encircling the presence of fear.

And so, I remain here, bound by time, nothing but time, only time.

Now there are only four tunnels ahead. I have to somehow move, get out of here.

I run to the first one and try to leave behind this fear.

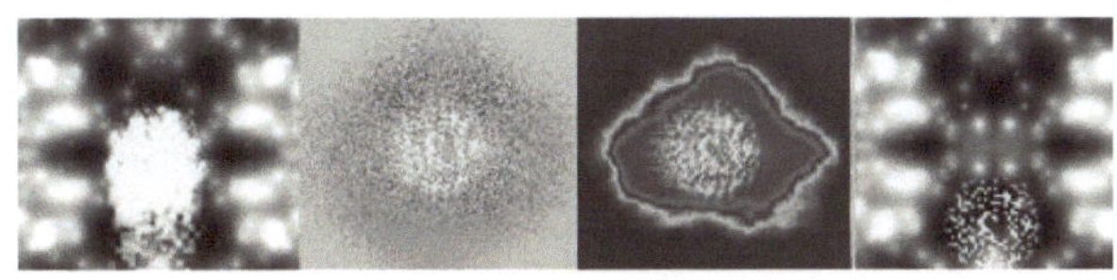

Futuristic Horizons

Is this the ultimate darkness, the coming of death; am I just searching for my soul, my place of rest or am I just caught up in some non-reality sub-plot, not funny, it's not.

Seems I'm just floating through some lonely, dark secluded passages, as the stillness closes in and walls collapse.

Memories, somewhat blurred, slowly emerge. I'm seeing faces I've known and places I've been. But, are these my memories, my feelings, my thoughts?

Still there is reasoning beyond doubt, my thoughts are scattered all about.

My mind is going in and out of its self; I'm in the past, the present and the future, all at the same time.

This just can't be!

I'm visualizing futuristic horizons, outer limits never before seen, with inner planetary objects, swirling and jutting out, nearby and overhead, all about.

There are dark horizons yet unearthed, ghastly experiments being secretly researched, scientists wondering who will be first.

I can see creations beyond thought, scary visions of the world, as it is and is not.

They, whatever they are or might be, seem to be amazed and bewildered at how it all began, the so-called beginning, the progress and evolution of man.

I run towards the tunnels, there are only three this time, I try the middle one, just to see, but the barrier doesn't let me flee.

I head to the first one and quickly leave.

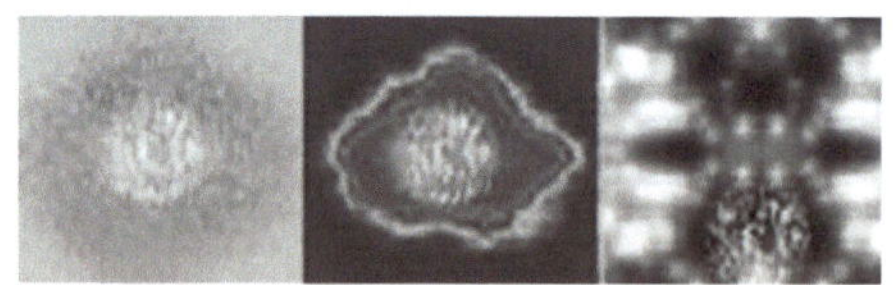

The Cold Aura

The saneness of my own being is being tested and is now touching and clutching at my very soul.

A reflection surges forward, standing out like it was borrowed and is now visualizing into life, into utter realization.

With one last hope of courage, I reach out to destroy it, that dark reflective image, but as my flesh touches the cold aura, a flashing bright haloed light shines and emerges, emitting the final calling.

But ...

I'm still here, still awake I think, still wondering; random thoughts bouncing in and out of my head, still alive, I can't be dead!

It's still dark everywhere, a dim faded light here and there.

What the hell did I do, what have I gotten myself into.

I can still feel that cold aura hanging about, chasing me down no doubt.

How do I escape its clutches, someone, anyone, get me out of here.

Suddenly I see a familiar face; hear a familiar voice. I yell, over here, over here!

No response. Everything just disappears.

Am I now imagining things, maybe hallucinating, or maybe one too many beers?

(*Oh what I'd do for a drink and a smoke right now!*)

There are a couple of tunnels ahead.

I wonder why the tunnels keep fading in numbers.

Oh well, I'm out of here.

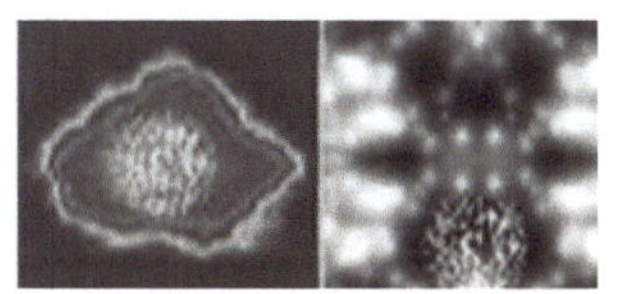

Befuddled and Confused

It's still quite dark here and strange noises everywhere.

I haven't seen light, real light, for so long, my eyes will never adjust, but I know it's a must.

I stay withdrawn, something is gnawing, yet I feel its presence known, something is glowing.

Here I am, awaiting the deafening sounds, reverberations yet to hear and find, with this thunderous shaking in my mind.

What was that? What did I just say? It felt like an earthquake or a volcano erupting in my head.

This really makes no sense at all; more like gibberish, all nonsense!

My minds been infected; I have no control, like something's been injected into my soul.

As I slowly descend on the task at hand, I try to find my way back to reality, back to a calmer land.

I stumble forwards and try to view which way to go; it's so dark, dank and cold here, I can hardly move.

My mind is wandering now, my vision blurred, I am still quite befuddled and most definitely confused.

A stretching imagination, running and drifting away, deep within the non-reality of thought, seeing the world as it is and is not.

Oh geez, there I go again, saying something about the world as it is and is not ... what does that even mean? Is it me talking or is someone inside my head, manipulating my thoughts?

Onward I trek, but so hard to breathe; the air is thick like fog, making it hard to proceed.

I see a passageway ahead and make my way to the entrance.

Oh let me rejoice, be the right choice.

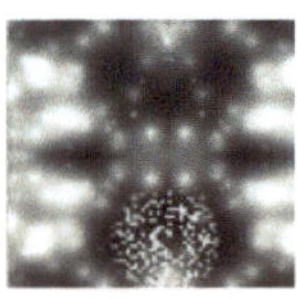

The Switches

What's this? A giant wall of some sort with a strange splash pattern; looks like it has a couple of switches above the letters L and R high on the wall; seems one is on the left and one is on the right. I guess I have to pull one of them, but wonder which one is right.

Suddenly I hear a gravelly voice (*okay, now I'm hearing bloody voices, what the hell is next*).

"*Make sure you pick the right one; there is only one right; do it right or you'll end up back here*".

The voice fades and I say to myself, "*who in god's name can that be*".

Not sure I understood what the hell he was saying but I guess I have a 50/50 chance here.

Umm, left or right...right or left? I reach up and pull the left switch.

There's a small flickering electrical spark; I jump back, let my eyes readjust and soldier on in a flash.

More Switches

Well that didn't get me anywhere, seems like I'm just up against another wall, maybe the same one, but it has a different pattern and three switches this time instead of just two; the letters L, C and R now appear vividly on the wall.

Suddenly I hear that voice again.

"I told you to do it right? There is only one right; do it right or you'll end up back here, and don't be the center of attention".

I think maybe I'm beginning to understand; yes, I've got it now.

He says do it right, there is only one right and don't be the center of attention. So that must mean, don't go left, don't go center, just go right.

I pull the right switch and this time there is a big flash of light radiating from the wall. I gather myself and continue onward.

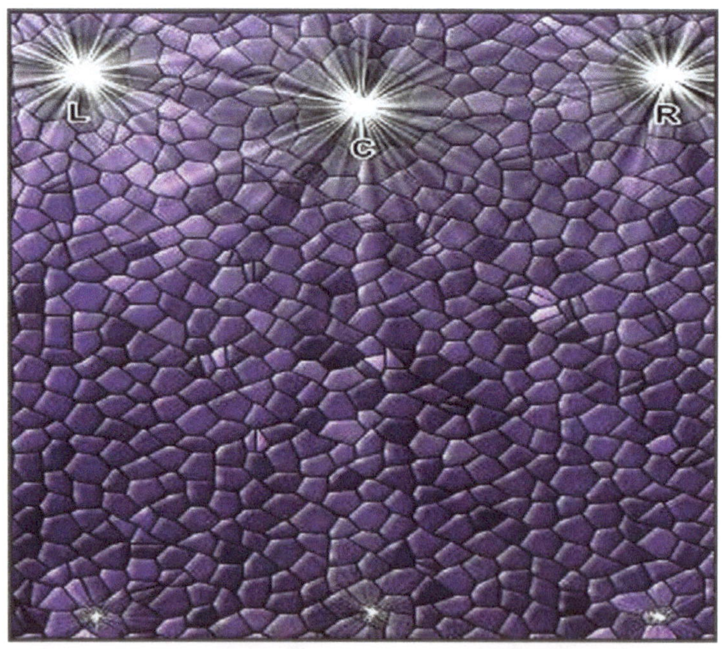

ROBERT R. BLONDIN

Poetry Land?

Well, I guess I made the right choice, as right as it can be! Maybe he, whoever the hell he is, was trying to tell me I should listen better, like that's really my problem here right now.

Okay, where am I now? Still pretty dark but at least I'm breathing easier. Oh please, someone, anyone, wake me up from here.

I see some shadows; I hear more voices but different this time; strange voices talking in rhyme, a different voice one at a time.

Is this a poetry reading, with all these voices in verse? Am I stuck in some kind of poetic conundrum, some oh so humdrum.

Is this a reading from Shakespeare, Browning, Longfellow and Frost, all poets of the past? Maybe it's all of them, each with a specific task. Not too sure though, never heard this stuff before.

The voices continue, different they be, each speaking one line at a time and all in rhyme.

Childish schemes, scattered dreams, everlasting feelings, unseen scars, still dormant in the dark canyons of my mind, slowly garnered, through the ages of time.

A stretching imagination, infectious in itself, now strewn and running amok, with spirits slightly numbed.

Deep set feelings emerging, surfacing, to and fro, dangling and dancing, as if jumping from an old dusty book.

Childish schemes, scattered dreams, everlasting feelings and unseen scars.

That was, uh, quite interesting, but still not sure what it all meant. Those are some great poets but they've come and gone; their time is all spent.

Was there a message here? Is it something to do with guilt feelings, cheating and lying? I'm not really sure what they were implying.

Oh well, looks like I'm back at the freaking beginning, I see all six tunnels again.

I must struggle on; maybe this one will get me out of this darkened domain.

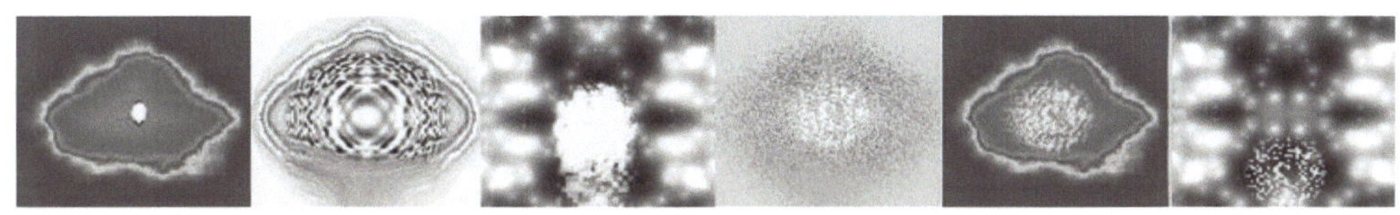

walls Closing In

Nope, not this one, damn it! Sure would like to wake up to some form of reality, but I keep following this darkened trail, a path of senseless idiocy.

Come on, someone, anyone, wake me up!

Mighty cold here, must proceed with upmost caution, must control my emotions, and control my wrath.

Are these walls closing in, or am I imagining things; it sure seems like a narrowing of the path.

I need to hurry, need to be quick, but my head still hurts, yet I can't quit.

I hear beckoning calls from beyond, from somewhere, maybe those walls closing in, making such a shrieking noise, engulfing my soul and my mind.

The deafening sound, like the hand of fate, slices right through the thick air, thrusts forward, reaches out, clutches and wrestles with my senses.

The ensuing gust turns me about, leaving me in hopeless despair.

Within the whispers of the frigid breeze, I can hear the sounds imposing, the beckoning sounds enclosing and those shuddering calls from beyond. It's such an eerie feeling, such an eerie tone; my senses dulled and almost completely gone.

But I know I'm still here, even though my brain seems scattered and I'm all alone.

I must move forward, find a way out, before these walls crush my being, my soul.

What's this? Looks like just five tunnels now; doesn't make any sense.

Every time I go through a tunnel, it gets eliminated, meaning I can never go back. The destination changes each time too, even when I repeat the process, six down to one, back to six. These openings always look the same, lesser at times, and nothing remains the same, it's always something anew, always a change.

Something has got to give; I enter the first one I see, now where will it lead.

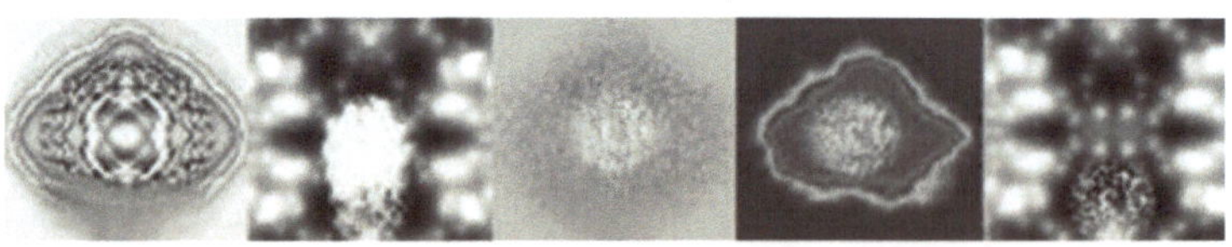

   ROBERT R. BLONDIN

A Face, A Smile

Okay, so this looks promising, I see a sort of calm here, is this reality? Am I finally out of this muddled chaos, this darkened distorted mess?

I see the faint image of a face, with a nice smile, but I don't know who it might be, my vision is still foggy, distorted and blurred.

A whispering breeze mentions a name, although I have no recollection, not sure who, although I see someone from my supposed past, just not sure of the name attached; maybe all of this is nothing more than deception, I have no real perception.

The beauty of that smile, that long flowing hair, visions drifting through, I forgot not to remember you.

You're with me, inside me, as I walk, you walk, as I talk, you talk, visions drifting through; I forgot not to remember you.

Your loveliness caresses my soul, as the mystics unfold, your spiritual presence, apparent and reaching out, now touching, feeling, existing, you're with me, inside me, and all because I forgot, I forgot not to remember you.

Oh I'm talking in gibberish again. Is someone or something trying to make me realize a truth or perhaps some mistake I might have made in the past?

Or does it have something to do with the people in one's life, maybe losing touch with old friends, family too.

Not sure how to interpret this, still not sure who she is or who she was; it's like I have no recall, no mental reception at all.

I do know I must move onward, although this is nice, the cold seems to have lessened and the darkness not a plight.

And, if going forward is somehow not right, maybe I can return here and spend the night, although these tunnels control my flight.

I must go on ... now only four.

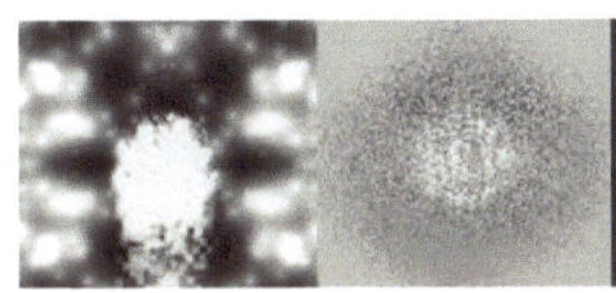
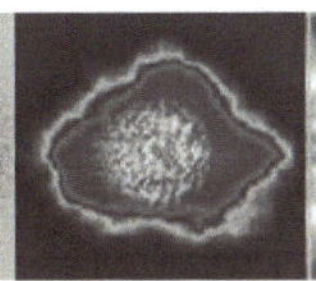
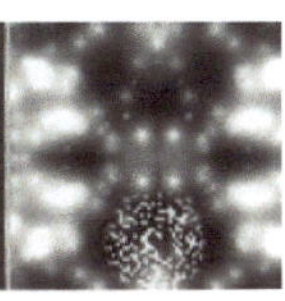

The Abyss

Damn, I've somehow stumbled along in this tunnel and I've now shown up here. This place doesn't look very intriguing, seems to be a dark sphere, with an unknown danger, soon to erupt.

All around, overhead and on the ground, there is a heavy fog with fragments of ice; hard to breath, not very nice. I can feel a presence near; is it the irony of fear?

Something unknown thrusts forward. It is like an invisible twine, entangling, tightening, choking and strangling me; I'm gasping for air, but all in despair.

This is so bizarre; I can still breathe, but just barely.

What did I get myself into here; it's like that other place, the past, the present and the future, all wrapped into one, this time it's around my neck, squeezing me senseless, making me dream within a dream, rather nightmarish it be.

I'm looking into an abyss, somewhere on this dark sphere; a dark hole of fate, emitting the wrath of fear. I have no feeling, no reality to speak of, and no control; have I lost my soul?

I find myself reaching into the dark emptiness, like the openness of outer space.

All of a sudden I'm editing tomorrow's headlines, I know all the unsaid predictions, I can see all the errors not yet made and I see the world moving at quite a fast pace.

I lift my head up from the abyss, tired and sore and I am now instilled with a darkened fear; never ever seen anything like this before.

Imagine being able to see things before they happen, being able to see and predict the future.

Maybe the unknown should remain unknown?

Right now I can remember all of this, what I'm seeing and what I'm hearing, but I still have no memory of myself.

The invisible hold on me is fading now; it's time to get the hell out of here, somehow!

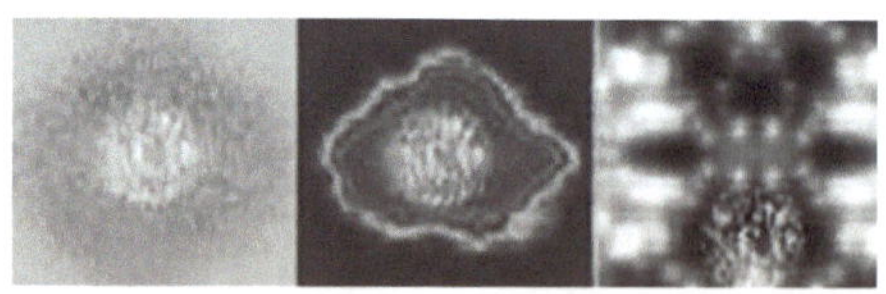

ROBERT R. BLONDIN

Can't Escape The Abyss

Oh no, did I just go in a circle or what. Seems this tunnel leads nowhere, I'm stuck in that dark abyss again. Or, maybe it's another one, another big dark gap in space, a hellish hole of fear it be.

What is going on? Someone please wake me up from this torment. Hey, anyone? Do you hear?

Seems like I've lost all control, must find a way out of this forsaken darkness, it's so dank and cold.

Peering into the darkness, the deepness of the abyss, looking for the simple truth, craving the inevitable, what's to be, seeking the realism of life and the awakening of life.

Wow, I don't even know what I'm saying, what is it I'm speaking, is my intelligence peaking? Am I thinking someone else's thoughts, they must be someone else's words, surely not mine.

Searching for a true tomorrow, the future of mankind, it all seems distorted in a blur; oh what will I find?

Is someone inside my head, playing with my thoughts; maybe someone dead, someone not?

Gee, now I'm watching some kind of sci-fi movie, like being caught up in the twilight zone or the outer limits; it's like nothing I've ever known.

I'm seeing visions of life's tragic trail, like up on a screen, from beginning to end, but it's unclear and so vague and so confusing, such a heart stopping fail.

What the hell did I breathe in from that hole? I seem to have lost my mind, lost all sense of control.

I'm hearing earthquakes not yet erupting, I'm speaking words not yet known, or never ever spoken.

My mind is filled with despair, darkness prevails, and my thoughts don't even seem to be mine, everything is so out of line.

Who am I? What am I? Where am I? What's happening to me this time?

Something is controlling me, but what!? Why the hell can't I just wake up?

I better keep moving, choose one or two, no time for snoozing,...

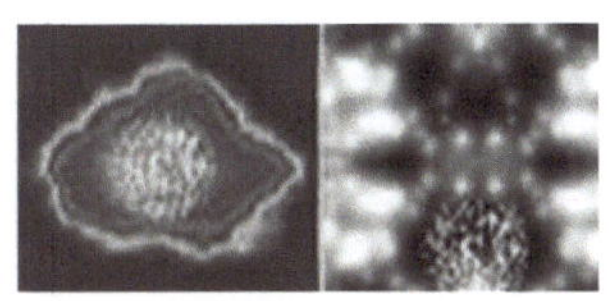

Calm Before The Storm

Okay, now this looks better; well, maybe, maybe not!

I find myself in this dark deserted area, seems to have a peaceful feeling about it, although it could be deceiving, like the calm before the storm.

Damn, felt like something just flew by me; oh so much for peace and tranquility.

Nothing seems to be here though; at least nothing I can see.

I tried to stay calm, sentimental I tried to be, but whatever it was, it surged forward and started strangling me; oh so hard to breathe.

Is this real or is my imagination just running wild? Maybe it was the guilt I had stored up inside, maybe something else; don't know for sure, I'm feeling a little down, a little riled.

Maybe I'm feeling someone else's guilt, maybe someone else's pain; these deep bedded feelings, too much to bear, can't be concealed, coming down on me like pouring rain.

I'm envisioning myself having these emotional outbursts, having no bodily control; nor a sense of real.

What is this, what's happening, what is this I feel?

Whatever it truly is, it gushed outwardly, flowing quite free, seems nothing can stop the onslaught; maybe only me.

What the hell is this, another kind of message, something to do with losing one's temper or controlling one's temper? Not too sure, surely not me, can't remember.

Besides, my memories are cloudy and faded, my brain filled with grey matter and my thoughts all in a tatter.

I need to take charge, need to find a clue, get myself back to reality, back to my own life, and all the things that really matter.

Only one opening ahead, I run quickly towards it, hoping this will end the dread.

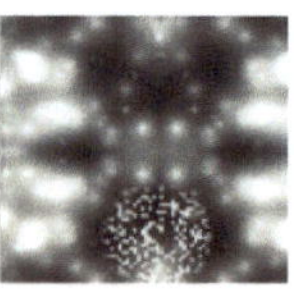

ROBERT R. BLONDIN

The Transporter Room

What have I got myself into now?

Normally, as if this is anywhere near normal, I'd be back at the beginning with all those six tunnels.

But it seems like I'm in some large room with a circular platform in the middle; it keeps spinning around and around and around; something like what's going on in my head.

I see a bunch of tube shaped passageways, like narrowing tube wires, all presumably leading to the center; but to the center of what? It has a flashing button near the entrance; maybe I can enter here by pressing the blinking button. Yes, okay, that did the trick, it stopped spinning real quick.

This contraption must be some kind of futuristic teleportation device, able to magically transfer you from one place to another. I'm not quite sure which tube shaped tunnel to take though? Hey you voices, help me out here will you?

Unexpectedly, a tube door opens and I have no choice but to enter, nervous and fearful I be.

The Relection

Wow, that was quite the trip; my head is still spinning, got to get a grip.

I'm now stuck inside something that reflects, something like glass, like a mirror, although foggy and cracked.

Within the mirror I see a face. Is it me or someone else? Or, is it something else?

Within my mind there is no trace or vision of what I see and the reverse reflection does not reveal anything to me.

It just seems to be a blank picture, perhaps a representation of how I feel.

I'm seeing a vision of nothing living, no sense of what the image is giving; it's just a face, without a trace, amid a glancing look into space.

I gaze into the mirror again and try to visualize, I take a closer look and now I realize, I'm seeing a vision of nothing living, it is just a blank face, without a trace, such an utter waste.

What was all that? What am I saying? Is it me thinking these thoughts?

Is there a message there; is it just gibberish or maybe an expression of truth, like 'what you see may not always be what you really need to see'?

It's time to move onward.

Sure wish I could be back in that teleportation room and just push a button that says 'home'.

Hey, look, all those damn tunnels again. I'm getting really tired of all this - someone, anyone, please wake me up!

Okay, I'm going to try one of those middle ones – oh damn, no such luck, an invisible barrier stops me in my tracks.

Again I can only enter the first one; I hope it takes me back home.

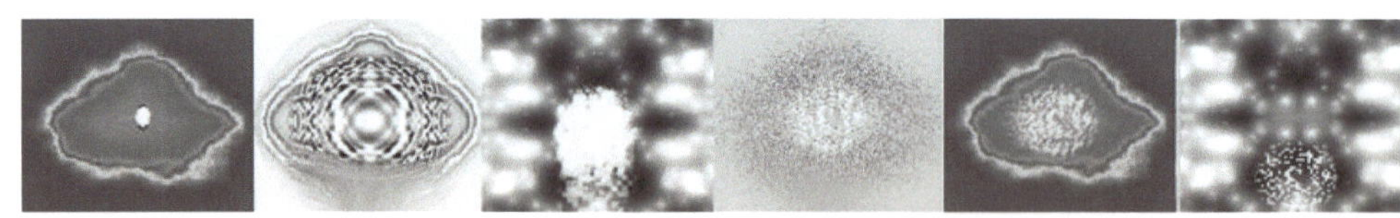

ROBERT R. BLONDIN

Thoughts – Down & Out

Damn it! Where am I now, still no light in sight? When is this going to end?

It's another day of utter loneliness, although I really don't know if it's really a day, there is no sense of time here, no sense of being, just no sense at all.

Nothing seems to be going right; I can see that in the stillness, the silence of the night, the darkness of plight.

Here I am, down and out and there is absolutely no doubt, I don't know what it's all about.

I'm seeing visions of nothing, hearing whispered words spoken, feeling down and quite heartbroken.

What's with all this strife? Is this my pain; is this my bane of existence, my bane of life?

Am I sensing someone else's hardship, someone else's pain?

The subdued aura, the quietness, the silence inflicting my mind, I'm pondering over what's to be, what's left behind.

Here I am, down and out; absolutely no doubt, I don't know what it's all about.

Geez, are these even my thoughts? Am I suffering from the dreaded thought nots?

Can't see clearly yet, but it is sure time to leave ... and look, five tunnels ahead, whoopee!

I know, take the first tunnel, lord knows I've tried them all.

Here goes ... let's see where I fall.

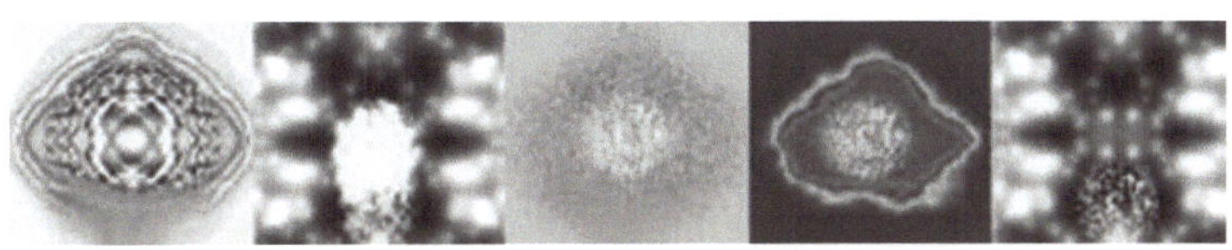

The Big Square

What is this? It's like a big square, dark but yet very colorful, as color here can be.

Seems like a large canvas of sorts and I'm trapped inside. What the ?

Is it a mosaic window or a painting of some kind? How can this be?

From a painter's point of view, the picture on the wall said it all. The curves and strokes of the brush, vibrating a titillating rush.

The vibrant color fast designs, with protuberant lines and shades of hue, create a perspective quite anew.

But, only a case of fiction, not fact, and if thou art confused, it must be abstract!

How the hell did I get into a painting? I'm stuck, how do I get out?

Maybe I need to find a brush and repaint from within?

Geez, where would I even find paint, let alone the brush?

I see something nearby, it looks like an eraser; perhaps I can use it to escape this thing.

Oh, wait, that might delete and obliterate me. Can't have that now, can we?

Oh what to do, what to do?

Maybe I can just move slowly, follow the curves and lines and get to the edge of the canvas, perhaps the edge of time.

I start to move, going slowly, one step at a time, bending at the curves and staying on the lines.

Yes, yes, that worked, I've made it out.

Okay, a tunneling I go ...

(did I just say that, I must be delirious from all the paint fumes)

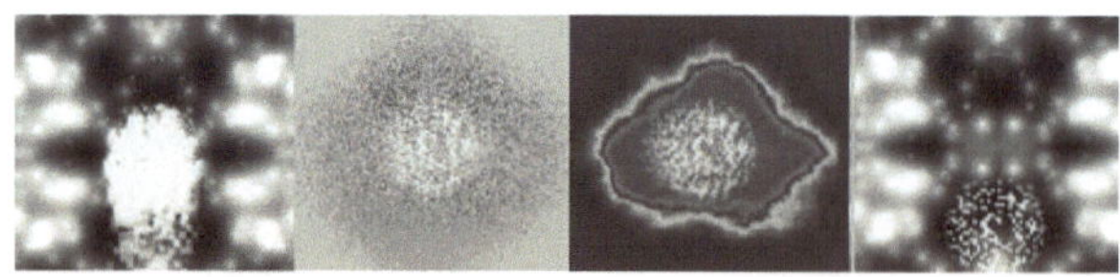

ROBERT R. BLONDIN

An Apparition

Still dark here but at least I have some sense of vision. I wonder what this place will bring, hopefully more than just indecision.

Unexpectedly, I am confronted by an apparition of sorts; it is like my previous encounter with 'that face, that smile', in that other place I thought was supposedly calm and tranquil.

It's a young lady, someone from my past, maybe my future, if I even have one still.

What the hell has happened to the present, my here and now?

Her eyes were a glittering green, with a bewildering gleam. Her hair was a golden hue, damp with a light touch of morning dew.

She stood in a shadow of her own making, as if there for the taking. The air had a scent of the wild, but yet, with a temperament, quite mild.

She raised her hand, motioning me forward.

I made a step, but froze, like a coward, I could sense an evil near, but my eyes could not see, and I could not hear.

I felt the excitement she created, the thrill she instilled in me. She was a silhouette outline, in the narrow path ahead, her piercing eyes paralyzing me; all my senses now dead.

Unconsciously I approached, with a cautious step, I knew I could not turn back, not now, not ever, not yet.

Her arms stretched out, embracing my soul; my excitement grew and then withdrew, and then, everything went cold, she had hold.

I seem to be in a trance, like under an evil spell; how do I get out, oh do tell.

Do I accept what is happening or find a way to flee from her clutches, her grasp.

Perhaps if I just try hard to open my eyes, maybe look away, I can release the grip of her hand.

Look away, look away; yes, yes, and so I ran and ran …

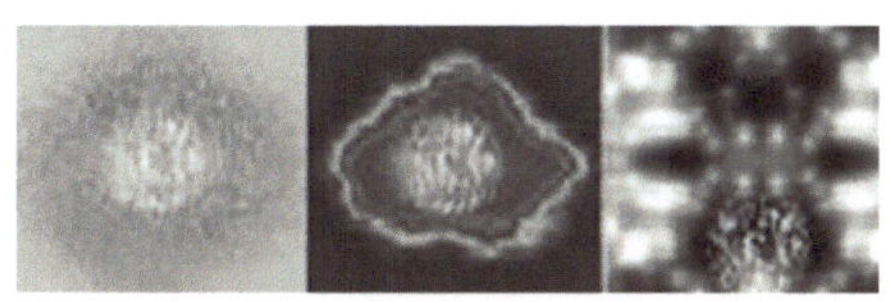

The Beach

Okay, now I am somewhere near a beach, I can hear water flowing and feel the sand under my feet; seems quite nice.

Is this my way out, maybe I can find a boat, make a raft or something; oh what the hell am I thinking, I can't even get out of this nightmare, let alone figure out how to build something.

Wake up damn it! Just wake up! Help, can anyone hear me?

Is this just another dark encounter, is something or someone going to jump out at me or am I finally going to gain consciousness and get back to reality, or will it just be another downer.

A nasty cool wind appears, creating a fortress in the sand; and from the formed gritty mound, comes the formation of a hand, stretching, reaching out, grasping for fulfillment.

Silent waves, the solemn soft wind blowing, clear blue water flowing, seeing a vision of someone on the sandy shore, but now disappearing, to be seen no more.

Fear instills my already trembling body, as the hand surges upward and forward, slowly approaching my soul, coming closer, closer, and closer, grasping for a piece of me, a small piece of reality, something I sure don't have much of right now.

An inner sense suddenly emerges and destroys my thinking, both reality and non-reality now linking, but I manage to open my eyes to the silent waves and the solemn soft wind blowing.

The hand starts to descend and quickly dissolves and returns to the earth, and I, without delay, run for the next passageway, just to get the hell away.

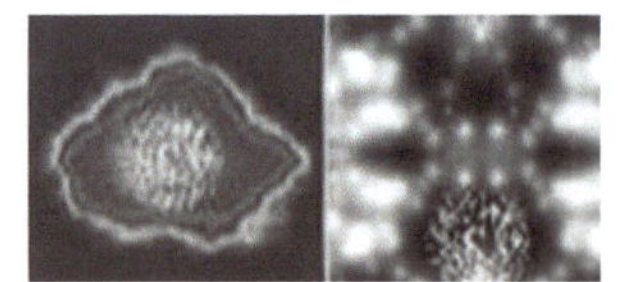

The Visitors

Not sure where I am now, still dark, no direct light in sight.

All I see around me are some things that resemble orbs; spheres flying to and fro.

What can they be? What can it mean?

All of a sudden I hear a voice coming from the distance, a voice from my past maybe, someone long gone but no one I recognize at this instant.

The voice is very pronounced and seems to be directed right at me.

I hear *'we are visitors', 'we mean you no harm'.*

And then I have all these words flashing through my mind, all in rhyme.

We come to you in thoughts, sometimes quickly, sometimes not.

We stay as long as we want, or, as long as you want; we sometimes even haunt, maybe just taunt.

We survive in memories, good or bad, you control the emotion, whatever the notion, and it's not meant to be a magic potion.

We sometimes appear as magical orbs, to which you see, sometimes shadows, white or black, even colors to confuse, all of this to simply give you a shivering flashback.

We come to you in thoughts, sometimes quickly, sometimes not!

These words all slowly fade from my mind and the voice dulls.

Well, at least this was something I didn't have to really run from, although it was still pretty creepy, deep and bizarre.

It didn't really sound like demons, perhaps my guardian angel from afar?

I still have this apprehension though, maybe its fear. (*Oh man, could I ever use a beer!*)

Only one tunnel ahead; okay, I'm out of here ...

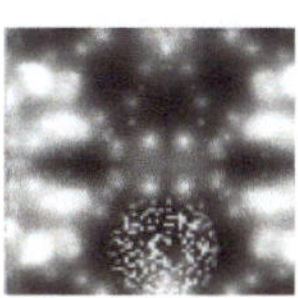

The Cavern

Seems I'm now in some kind of cavern, a grotto of sorts, a dark cave with a blue misty tint.

Ahead in the shadows there appears to be people, mysterious they be; maybe they can help me escape, at least give me a hint.

Oh geez, what am I talking about, this is not some kind of video game here, just let me wake up will you?

I see the shadowy outline of two, talking back and forth, like on cue.

As I approach, I get this eerie feeling as their voices echo to and fro; not sure whether I should stay or just go.

Suddenly I hear the voices, in sync, saying *'darkness is only in your mind, turn your thoughts into bright light and escape you might'*.

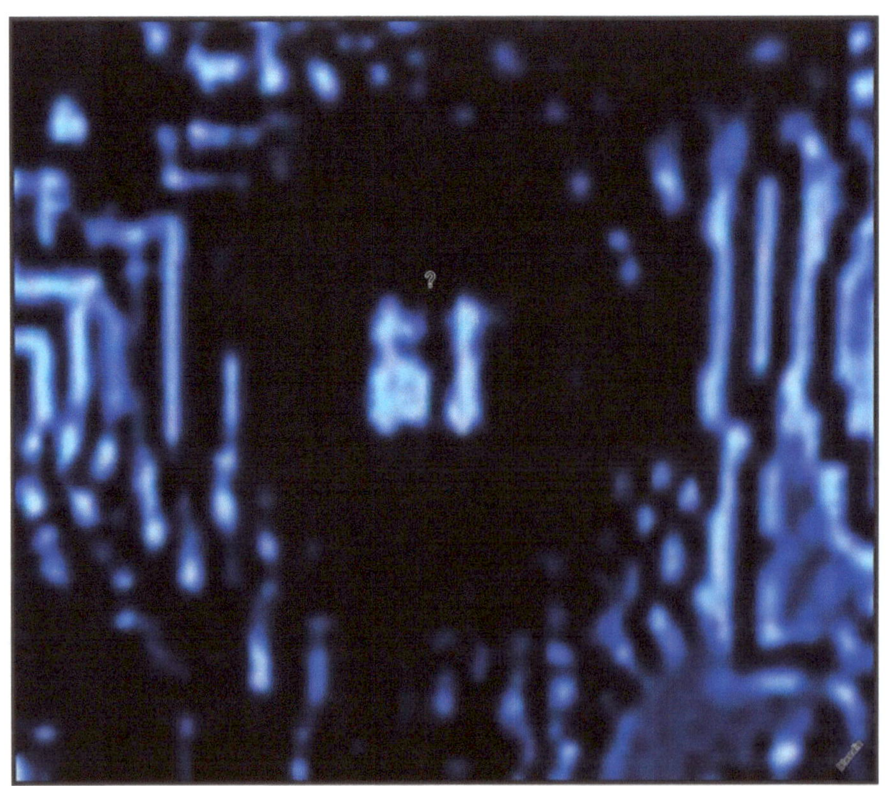

Hallucinations

Okay, so I'm thinking bright thoughts but what in the world is this? There is darkness but yet colors are bouncing around all over the place and flashing lights are flickering in and out of sight.

Have I been drugged? Maybe that's what's wrong with me; maybe someone slipped me something without me knowing. Wait, it's hard to remember but I thought I just went for a nap; I wasn't out partying that I know of; oh crap!

Now I'm seeing what looks like a giant television or movie screen, with flashing words being read out to me.

It's that gravelly voice again and I hear:

Perspective dreams, with cowardly schemes, sudden characteristics changing, lives shuffled and rearranging.

Pictorial patterns, filled with golden Saturns and pixilated people vividly feeble.

Just fabrications of your mind, concepts and visual memories, caught up in a quandary of time, and so drastically benign.

Oh, it was some kind of high!

What the!? What was that all about?

Sounds like someone is high on something and hallucinating no doubt.

Is it me? Who, me? Surely not me!

What's he trying to tell me? Stay away from drugs; stop taking drugs?

Like, okay, okay? Just let me wake up will you.

Look, all those damn tunnels again, maybe I'll get the right one this time.

Let's cross the threshold and see.

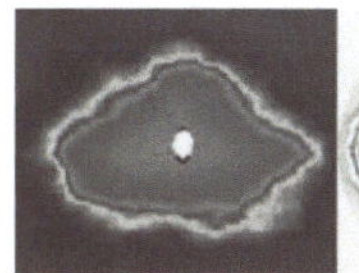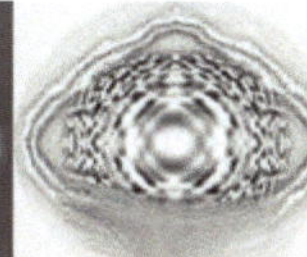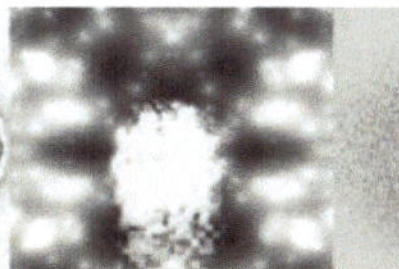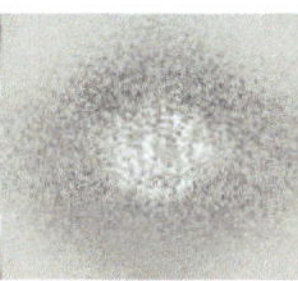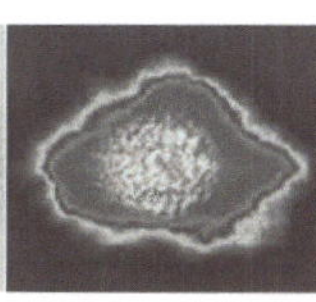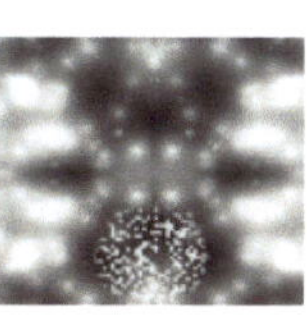

The Land Of Guilt

Peace is but the subsiding of pain, hurt is but the creation of guilt; guilt is but only a feeling, deep within the subconscious being.

What? What the hell is that, where am I now?

And, gee, they are talking about guilt again, like that's my problem here.

Someone please wake me up! Hello, anybody out there!?

Suddenly I hear that gravelly voice again and I hear it in an arrangement of rhyme.

Times are hard and times are tough, be happy, you've got more than some, yet, wishing and hoping for more, no one ever has enough.

To be one with one is not to run, you are damn fortunate to be one.

This ever changing world we live in, your life rearranging, melodies playing, reaching for the utmost, remember, don't boast, just coast.

To be one with one is not to run, you're fortunate to be one.

Your life is your life, but don't forget, others have a share, so don't take it away, others care, they really do care.

To be one with one is not to run, yes, you're damn fortunate to be one!

What is he talking about now? I am who I am, fortunate or otherwise. I haven't done anything stupid that I know of.

Am I dead or what? Oh, damn, what the hell did I go and do? I just took a nap, a simple little nap; I can't remember anything prior to.

All I know, at this moment, is that my fortunes aren't very good; I'm stranded here in this dreaded darkness, the darkness of thought, and I'm alive, I think!

There must be a way out, have to keep searching, just keep going; one of these tunnels has got to be my escape route.

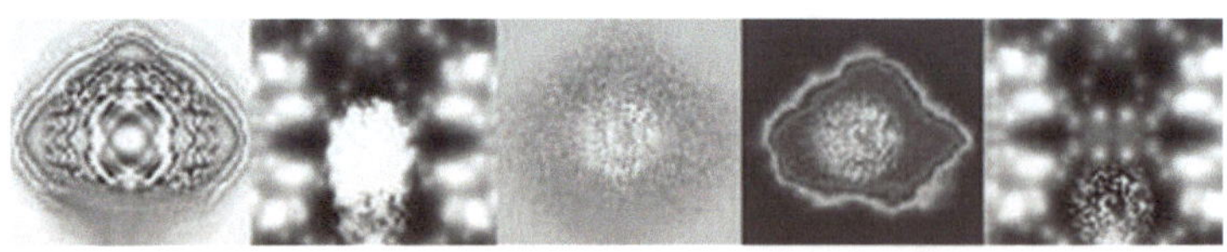

Don't Carry Life & Offer Revenge

Now where am I?

Someone is there, not sure who, outlined in a shrouded veil of darkness with a purplish hue, housed in the dark shadows shaded with blue.

I hear a voice from within; not the same gravelly voice I'm use to.

Is this all in my head, am I just dreaming, am I maybe dead.

Is this perhaps my demons, deep down inside, trying to send a message for me to decipher and justly abide. And, if that's the case, I must still be alive!

The voice seems friendly but I still have fear, an apprehension not quite clear.

Creation is but the pain of ecstasy, the suffering you must bear; you can surely see, by eyeing your past, the shame doesn't have to last and last, be at peace with thy soul; accept, care and share.

Don't carry life and offer revenge, the birth of life is what we yearn, and to err is but to learn.

Nothing is quite the same as love's pain, the great feeling of new life, one within one.

So, don't carry life and offer revenge, your actions were but hardcore dramatics, an immature reason for getting your kicks.

Always reach out for a warm hand, an understanding heart, a kind and gentle soul; don't carry life and yet offer revenge.

And who am I, I'm but a friend!

The voice fades. Where the hell are all these voices coming from, are they just all in my head?

Is it someone from the here and now, someone from the future, perhaps from my past? Who?

And, was this another one of those messages, something about birth and blame? Oh the shame!

Okay, well it all sounds fascinating, quite profound I say, but friendly or not, I've got to get away.

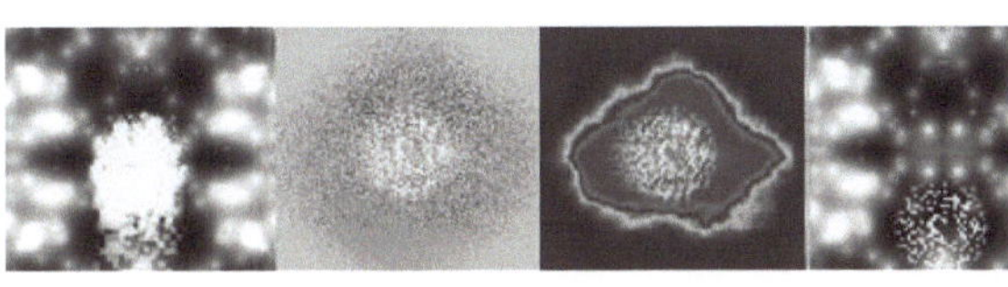

Waiting & Hoping

Now, let me see where I am, not that I can, this darkness still prevails over me.

This place is barren, desolate, dark and dank it be.

I hear a ruffling in the breeze; is someone there, or is it just me.

I hear a voice, another different voice it be, but no one I see.

The tone of the voice seems to be a mix of evil and good, and confused between could, should and would.

I yell out that I'm getting tired of all this; just say it please, I can't see you but speak if need be.

Suddenly I hear what sounds like a rhyme, a tempo of blues, from sad to glad, with back and forth views.

A song in my heart and no one to listen, longing, waiting and hoping, for what?

I'm empty, I'm stiff; my heart keeps pounding, feelings running adrift.

Visions sad and visions glad; not sure what I have, what I might have had.

Where am I and what am I - here alone, not quite content, hollow, incomplete and fully spent.

Bring to me the one I love, we'll sing our love song, until the day we're gone; hold me, touch me, breathe for me, with me, caress my soul, be with me; for you I'll wait, my strength is great.

And the voice pales away. Again, is it someone from my past, maybe from the future, or maybe someone dead? I just don't know who it could be. And, gee, is this just all in my head or am I the one that's dead?

And, what's with all the freaking messages?

Wait, if they, whoever they are, keep giving me messages, then I must still be alive, mustn't I?

Well, interesting and deep it all be, I must flee and escape all this misery.

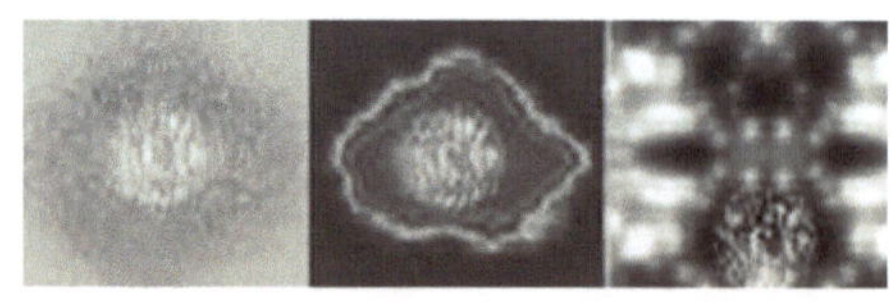

Poetry Land, Again!

Wow, looks like I'm back here in poetry land, the poet's corner of the world or whatever they call this crazy poetic place.

It seems most of the destinations I've been to, have some kind of rhyme, or reason; must be the poet's season.

And so I hear all those voices again, like before, and they are all in sync and quite distinct.

They are in harmony, like a choir singing a song; the words though, are deep and dark; oh hark, definitely not the sound of a singing lark.

Not sure what I'm hearing, but at least I don't feel threatened, there is no fearing.

The voices continue in harmony one line at a time.

Drifting fever of love, everlasting feelings, through the ages of time, holding onto only a fraction that is mine, awaiting the deafening sound, yet to hear and find, knowing the thunderous shaking, the pounding in my mind.

Widening landscapes of the universe, populations exploding, unkind and treacherous people within, all just making it worse.

Your stretching imagination running away, deep within the non-reality of thought, seeing the world as it is and is not; happiness, wishfulness, and then, the unsaid death, silence.

To be at peace within the saneness of life, the reality of being, the true reality of life, sometimes the answer is just too hard to find, knowing the guilt, the guilt within the depths of your mind.

The voices slowly fade.

Sounds like something from that other place, 'The Land Of Guilt' it was called. This was also quite interesting and pretty deep, but not sure what it all meant; maybe a message about the downfall of mankind and future generations maligned? Was it directed at me; if so, like everyone else, guilty I be.

Well, time to leave. I've been going in circles for so long now, back and forth through all these tunnels, such an endless plight; I sure hope the proper exit is in sight.

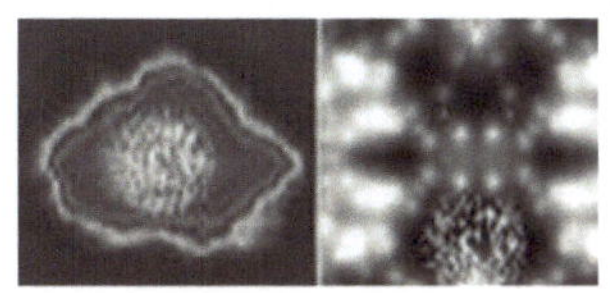

Tears From Heaven

Looks like I'm stuck inside some kind of dark bubble now; this could really spell trouble.

Seems to have a gentle touch though, not threatening much. And now it feels like pouring rain coming down on me, a warm sensation it be.

I don't feel at all wet though; it's like there is an umbrella over me?

Without any warning, I hear a familiar voice, yes, that gravelly voice again, reciting to me.

Inner feelings creeping, loving tears seeping, glaring, glimmering eyes upon you, holding back the tears, for a man does not cry, don't ask the reasons why, it's something grown in a man, since way back when.

Gee, maybe it's not rain at all, maybe its tears coming down, maybe tears from heaven? And, who is this guy with the gravelly voice? He sure is haunting me.

He grumbles and continues to recite.

A man's feelings should never be expressed, never second-guessed; a leader and protector he must be, the tears we should not see, for if he does weep and cry, he must give excuses, reasons why; inner feelings creeping, loving eyes seeping, glaring eyes upon you. Why?

The gravelly voice fades out.

Are all these strange destinations reflecting some kind of message? This one is all about a man crying, when he should, when he shouldn't; how does all this affect me?

The voice suddenly grumbles again.

It is quite normal for a man to cry; when he loses a loved one, a loved pet, when he gets married, when he becomes a father or when he totals his very first car; yes, whenever he wants to!

The voice dies away, releasing me from the bubble. I run quickly, hoping to find my freedom, and hopefully no more trouble.

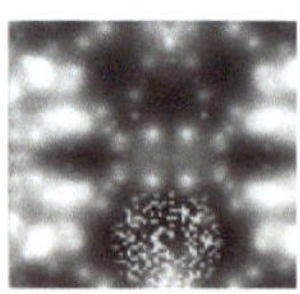

ROBERT R. BLONDIN

The Crystal

Now what? Looks like some kind of gigantic rock formation, a super sized crystal, quite the creation?

A stunning bright multi-colored light is emanating from it, oh so bright it be, surging with super powered electrical energy.

I hear a voice, that old gravelly voice again, still stalking me.

"Each sorrow or great happiness, is only what you scrounge, beg or borrow; to live a life is not to rest, beyond is what you shall truly live; a wondrous, glorious sight, pure as crystal and natural as light".

As the voice fades away, the light gets brighter and brighter and brighter.

Whats happening now, it's so bright, I can't see, I can't see!

I feel a radiant warmth as the crystal implodes, drawing me full force into it's light; this I can't fight.

Return Journey

Wow, I travelled right through that crystal and wound up here, whatever here might be. My vision is somewhat better now, going from bad to fair. There seems to be a lot of confusion and a strange noise in the air.

What is this ... a massive looking sphere, circling right in front of me, a sort of mechanical beast and so intricate in design. It goes to the left, then goes to the right, continues to change directions and seems to be controlling something, as I thought it might.

There seems to be an enormous number of circles, circles within circles, circles with more circles and numbers, high to low, low to high, going on and on. They are all moving in different directions, to and fro, never the same; they always change, repeating a rhythm, it's quite the mechanism. They all seem to stop and start, each circle and number playing a complex and elaborate part, with a large dark off-ramp as the exit and a smaller bright white on-ramp as the start.

Wow, confusing or what; I wonder what it all means? And why is this in my thoughts?

Looks like each set of circles and numbers follow a path of growth, small to large, back to small, then again to large, like the evolution of man, the birth of life; from beginning to end, and back again. Sounds just like life's journey; a return journey of sorts, from birth to death and back again. Is this everyone's life wrapped up in a bunch of freaking circles; is this the circle of life?

Suddenly I get these shivers trembling through my body and feel something hovering overhead. I hear that distinct gravelly voice again; oh why is he stalking me?

I, the one that is born, I, the one that breathes, I, the one that lives, I, the one that dies,

I, the one that is reborn!

So it is the circle of life as I thought. But, what is it trying to tell me? And, why me?

Oh look, there is only one opening ahead, usually it would be six. And this time it looks different.

I see water rippling, a bright light and a long white bridge. Seems to look safe, I wonder where it leads?

Have I finally escaped all those six tunnels? I take a deep breath, cross my fingers and cross over

(oh, maybe I shouldn't have used that term).

Scattered Space

What's this? It's not what I expected, like I really expected any of this to begin with.

Seems like everything is strewn and scattered, to and fro.

And what do I hear, it's that gravelly voice again (oh he is definitely harassing me).

'When you're feeling down and your mind feels cluttered and rather scattered, look up to see the way'.

Is he giving me a sign; seems to be a lot of messages today, if this is even a day; I have absolutely no sense of time.

Okay, I'm looking up as I walk straight through all this scattered clutter.

The Paths

Seems I'm now in some area with a lot of paths, zigs and zags, like some kind of obstacle course; how will I know where to go, which path do I take? I'll just have to take a guess here, I've been doing that for a quite a while now, haven't I.

Is this something like 'I'll cross that path when I come to it'?

Or maybe, 'we'll cross paths again someday'?

Or, perhaps it's something like 'one day you'll find your chosen path in life'.

Messages and more damn messages! Can I please just wake up and get on with my life?

I feel totally exhausted, totally lost, but here goes, like taking a hidden path through the park in the dark, as dangerous as that might be.

The Glob

Okay, made it out of there; felt like something was guiding me through all those paths.

Now where am I? What is this? Looks like a big glob like bubble ahead of me.

It looks like it is surrounded by a protective mist, with a lot of stepping stones within.

The mist seems to be a gated barrier, like all those other tunnels I could never enter.

With deepened fears, I push my hand forward into the mist and out of the blue, an opening appears.

Now I need to choose my way wisely, take one step at a time, tread ever so lightly.

Damn, is this another lesson in the making?

Oh well, here goes ... one stepping stone at a time *(oh another cliché!)*

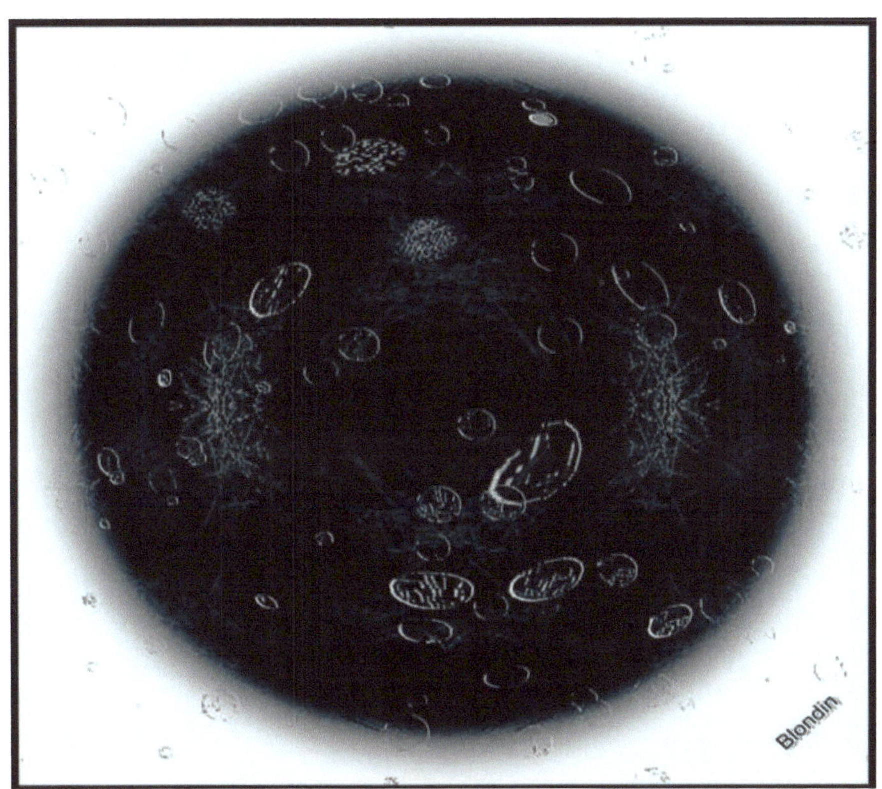

Our World

Again it felt like something helped me with those stepping stones; as I proceeded, each of them, the correct ones, kept illuminating ahead of me, letting me know where to put my feet.

Well, now it looks like I'm facing up at the world, our earth I guess, although it looks a lot different somehow; is it imploding? Looks fairly dark and dreary, still with a blue hue, but not very nice, not nearly.

What have we done, have we finally misused all there was to misuse, have we simply abused all there was to abuse.

Suddenly I hear that gravelly voice again.

'Change your ways, change your ways, or this will be the outcome and nothing shall remain'.

Okay, another message I guess. I look up and away and head onward.

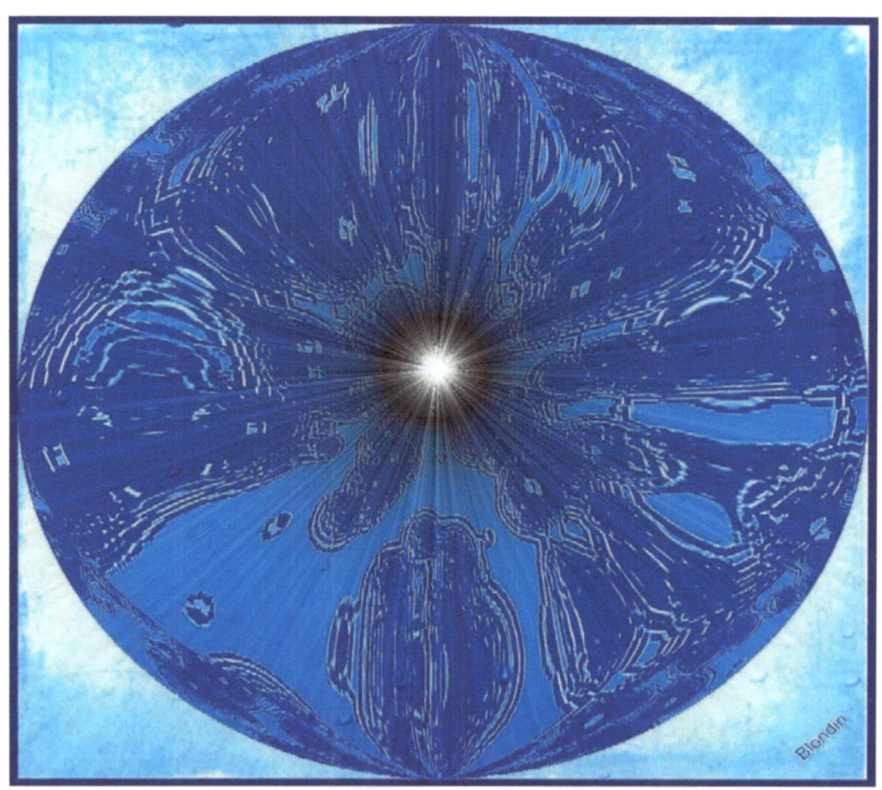

Recovery Phase

Looks just like before, although brighter, is it finally exploding or maybe going through a recovery phase, fixing all the things mankind has managed to abuse, misuse and screw. Can it simply be fixed on cue?

Let's move on, got to wake up from here.

I'm tired and sore, and I sure don't want to hear 'Mr. Gravelly's' voice anymore!

The Wall Panel

Wow, look at this!

Seems to be a big wall panel with numbers from one to six, just like all those tunnels I've been through before. I wonder what it does and what's it for.

Maybe it means I can return to all those previous locations I've been to? Now, why in hell would I want to do that?

But, I wonder, can I return to the beginning of my ordeal and escape this dread or would I just end up starting all over again and still be lost in the darkness of thought; can't take the chance of that happening now, can I.

Doesn't look like I can go forward from here, I need to make a choice.

Okay, let's see what happens when I press a number.

Wow, each time I press one it shows a vivid picture of where I've been; definitely don't want to return to any of those loony bins, except maybe that place where I saw a nice face and a smile, although I don't know who it was; it was still kind of nice and calm, and not threatening at all.

So, if I hit that number, it might take me there.

As soon as I press my choice, I am drawn into the middle of the panel, amid a flash of bright light.

Return To A Face, A Smile

Well, looks like I'm back here and all still looks clear, no fear, just that unknown face with a nice smile.

The wall panel was like a time machine I guess, but not very selective, only a few locations, more or less.

I still wonder though, could I have returned to reality by choosing the very first door I started through? Oh how I wish I knew.

Oh well, my choice was made, I have to live with it - that's if I'm even alive.

Okay, let me wake up now, please!

This place is nice, still has a calming feeling, with a pleasant sense of healing.

I can still feel the nice breeze and I don't hear any whispers this time.

It's like this place was the only one that wasn't extremely dark, cold, noisy, or threatening, but yet it doesn't seem to be my escape route, oh woe is me, not meant to be.

Why the hell can't I just get back to normal?

Look, there's that bridge again, the one with the water and the bright light.

I guess I have no choice but to cross it and see where it leads, hopefully I don't have to start all over from here.

Freedom?

Oh good, I didn't have to start over from all those other dreary places I've been.

Okay, this is so different, nice and calm too, much more light and less fright.

Could this be the one; have I finally escaped my darkened plight, this endless gloom and doom.

It seems I've been lost for an eternity, lost in the darkness of thought.

Is this really freedom? Am I back to reality, whatever normality has got?

Will I have all my memories back? Will I even remember this? Do I even want to?

Okay, going through now ... can't wait ...

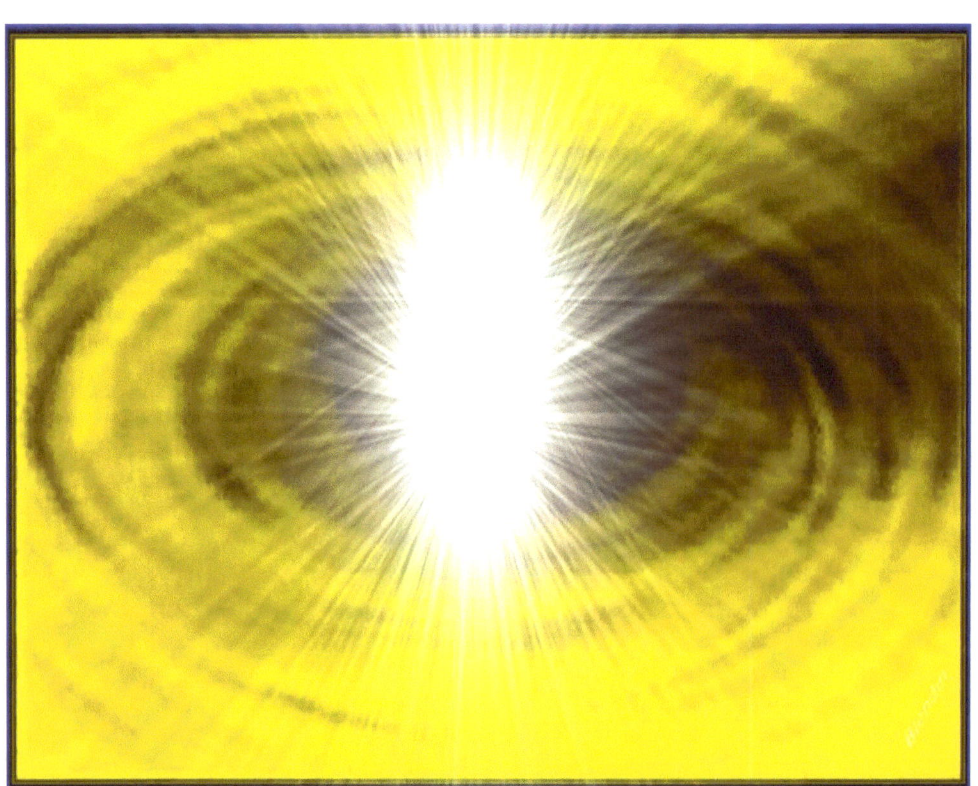

The Damn End?

Wow, that was such a brilliant bright light; I feel a strong energy emerging in me.

Is the darkness now over, finally over for me; oh the damn end it ought to be.

I'm sure to wake up now, right?

Come on, where are all those damn voices when you need them; someone just say 'right'.

Oh woe is me, nothing, just silence!

Yet, I'm not sore anymore, my head seems clear, my vision restored.

Just wake up, I implore!

Suddenly I hear a ringing noise, over and over and over, getting louder and louder and louder.

'Rrrring, Rrrring, Rrring'

Startled, I jump up and yell ... *'what the hell is that'*?

Blurry eyed and confused, I reach for the ringing phone and say *'hell-hello'*.

At the other end there is silence and a buzzing sound and then I hear:

'You need to come back down to the hotel, the lights keep flickering off and on and we're all in the dark here, you need to go see the hotel manager waiting for you on the main floor, his name is 'Mr. Gravelly'.

I said *'Oh my god, mister who?'*

Everything went dark, as I collapsed and fainted ...

Afterword

After I recovered somewhat, I realized I had finally awakened and escaped the dreaded darkness of my nap; still quite confused, still in shock, but alive I be.

My memories were still faded and blurred, but I seem to remember the name, Mr. Gravelly; like it was somehow etched permanently into the depths of my mind.

I promptly went down to that old rundown hotel with the antiquated electrical system I thought I had fixed.

I couldn't find the manager anywhere, but I noticed the lights back on and a letter for me at the front counter:

The letter read:

The power has been restored.
The circuit breakers for floors 1 to 6 kept moving up and down on their own;
Whatever the actual cause remains unknown.
I've assigned someone to watch the door.

The following words were signed in large letters directly below:

*G*uard *O*n *D*uty

Your friend,
"Mr. Gravelly"

Okay, I'm going right back home and going straight to bed .... umm ... maybe not!!

(?)

Remember to always say 'goodnight', like I was taught, you just never know what may happen when you enter into the darkness of thought!

Robert R. Blondin
bobmeistersplace.com
bobmeisterb@gmail.com